To Kevin

Love Palmer
7 Oct 2005

Happy Birthday

AUSTRALIAN FLOWER FAIRY VERSE

Birthday Book
Margaret Thornton
Illustrated by Elizabeth Alger

First published in 1993 by
Egan Publishing Pty. Ltd.
P.O. Box 283
Bentleigh, Victoria 3204.

ISBN 0 947272 91 7

Egan Publishing
Melbourne
Australia

Australian
Flower Fairy Verse
Birthday Book

Dedicated to the memory of
my loved and loving parents
Margaret Thornton and Stewart Thornton

Cecilia Egan.

COOTAMUNDRA WATTLE
(Acacia baileyana)

When Winter days are gloomy
And Spring seems never to come —
I will give you courage.

Look again in that dark corner,
And you'll be amazed to see
A coverlet of softest gold —
Dipping and dancing and laughing
To cheer the days of Winter cold.

My flowers light the grey-brown land
All through the year.
We are busy fairies — but
You should be glad we're here.

Margaret Thornton

Cootamundra Wattle

GUM TREES
(Eucalyptus spp.)

What does a gum tree look like?
In the snow it's small with coloured branches.
In the forests it is straight and tall.
Along the river banks
*   the red gums own*
*   the secret world*
*   that water birds call home.*

One thing each gum tree has
*   wherever it may grow*
*   are thousands of scented flowers*
*   from white to red*
*   offering their sweet honey*
*   till all the birds are fed.*

Margaret Thornton

Gum Trees

WATERLILY

(Nymphaea gigantica)

The pale blue waterlily blooms
   from the black mud of the lagoon.
Out of this sticky mess
   come plants of delicate finesse.
Swaying in the tropical warmth,
   they're like a tiny world —
   home to insects day and night
who use it as a rest from flight.

The fairies love their pale blue flower
   and guard it with their strength and power.
They use its floating, plate-like leaves
   as a platform for their fun and games;
   diving from the dark green edge —
   which makes a most convenient ledge —
   splashing and laughing as they play;
   it's like a picnic every day.

Margaret Thornton
17/9/92

Waterlily

JANUARY

1.

2.

3.

4.

5.

6.

7.

8.

9.

10.

11.

12.

13.

14.

15.

16.

JANUARY

17.

18.

19.

20.

21.

22.

23.

24.

25.

26.

27.

28.

29.

30.

31.

BROWN BORONIA
(Boronia megastigma)

Fragrance is my gift.
With quivering wings I shake the tiny bells,
Sombre green and yellow.
A perfumed cloud surrounds the quiet
* brown bush.*

You do not see me, but I'm there,
Tending my charge with loving care.

Margaret Thornton

Brown Boronia

FAIRY BELLS
(Sarcochilus ceciliae)

I grow on mossy trees
in the heart of the ancient forest.
Though hard to find,
my orchid flowers
vie with the fairies in their bowers.

Growers, take great care
of the exquisite tiny plants.
They are far away from their forest home
where human beings are unknown.
The fairies give them help and advice,
knowing their beauty
is beyond price.

Margaret Thornton

Fairy Bells

FEBRUARY

1.

2.

3.

4.

5.

6.

7.

8.

FEBRUARY

9.

10.

11.

12.

13.

14.

15.

16.

17.

18.

19.

20.

21.

22.

23.

24.

25.

26.

27.

28.

29.

DAMPIERA AND
BLUE LECHENAULTIA
(Dampiera linearis and Lechenaultia bilboa.)

Think of the bluest blue a flower could be.
I'd give you Dampiera —
*   or else its kissing cousin Lechenaultia.*
Let's talk of Dampiera — named for a pirate
*   who landed for fresh water in the west*
*   many years ago.*
He left his name for a fan-shaped,
*   five-petalled flower.*

After centuries of obscurity, its heavenly blue
*   still weaves enchantment, as is its due.*

Margaret Thornton

As blue as the depths of a summer sky,
*   as sapphire or lapis lazuli;*
Lechenaultia's vibrant hue
*   is the very essence of all things blue.*

Cecilia Egan

Dampiera and Blue Lechenaultia

YELLOW EVERLASTING DAISY

(Helichrysum bracteatum)

Flower of the sun!
Your golden petals
shine towards the sky.
A wheel of light
That opens when the dawn is nigh.

Thickly pleated from their central ring
your glowing yellow flowers
could outshine a king.

Margaret Thornton

Yellow Everlasting Daisy

MARCH

1.

2.

3.

4.

5.

6.

7.

8.

MARCH

9.

10.

11.

12.

13.

14.

15.

16.

MARCH

17.

18.

19.

20.

21.

22.

23.

24.

25.

26.

27.

28.

29.

30.

31.

THE GIPPSLAND
WARATAH

(Telopea oreades)

Would you expect to see
Deep in the forest's gloom
A tree adorned by radiant flowers
Glowing red, with life-attracting powers?

The fairies have to work with all their might.
The Waratah needs care; it's skilfully formed.
Its roots embrace the rich,
  dark Gippsland soil —
To grow it well takes dedicated toil.

Now we must say goodbye to this
  bright beauty.
We've shared its secret life —
Heard it singing songs of praise
Under the fairies' loving gaze.

Margaret Thornton

The Gippsland Waratah

COASTAL TEA-TREE

(Leptospermum laevigatum)

Fairy pies — who will buy my fairy pies?
My honeyed flowers, white as drops of snow,
nod amongst my perfumed leaves,
kissed by bees
and ocean breeze.
And when my flowers, fair of face,
should fade — what shall take their place?
Why, fairy pies, round and neat —
but not to eat.
Take care,
tea tree seeds lie sleeping there
in pies sliced evenly into eight,
ready to spill forth and propagate.
Where the long beach lies, salt wind sighs
and seagull cries ...

Cecilia Egan

Coastal Tea-Tree

APRIL

1.

2.

3.

4.

5.

6.

7.

8.

9.

10.

11.

12.

13.

14.

15.

16.

17.

18.

19.

20.

21.

22.

23.

24.

25.

26.

27.

28.

29.

30.

CLEMATIS
(Clematis glycinoides)

A shower of shining stars
    gleams in the damp brown gully —
    shielding the possum's home
    and bush-bird's nest.
Veiled by stitches of creamy white,
    finer than a tapestry,
    it brings delight to all who see.

Margaret Thornton

Clematis

THE CRIMSON BOTTLE-BRUSH

(Callistemon citrinus)

Callistemon — a simple, pretty name
for spiky, silken blooms of blushing flame.
Their shape resembles brushes used to clean
the inner sides of bottles. But their green
and crimson splendour is required instead
to grace the bushland and your flower-bed;
and elfin children use these blossoms fair
for tickling birds, or brushing fairies' hair.

Cecilia Egan

The Crimson Bottle-Brush

MAY

1.

2.

3.

4.

5.

6.

7.

8.

9.

10.

11.

12.

13.

14.

15.

16.

MAY

17.

18.

19.

20.

21.

22.

23.

24.

25.

26.

27.

28.

29.

30.

31.

TRIGGER PLANT
(Stylidium gramminifolium)

These charming spikes of flowers
capture the unwary traveller —
ant, bee or beetle —
Stylidium's trigger holds it tight.
The prisoner struggles, kicks, is painted with
a patch of pollen —
life-giving for fertile seeds
in neighbouring plants.
The footloose wanderer is then allowed
to leave.

Our tiny Romeo
staggers off to other spikes
(hasn't learnt his lesson!)
and climbs a similar bloom
where he falls into the trap again
and struggles ...

Margaret Thornton
18/9/92

Trigger Plant

WAX FLOWER
(Hoya australis.)

They look not like real flowers at all,
   but like stars, perfect and small,
   moulded from white candlewax; or fakes
   formed from sugar frosting
   to decorate cakes.

But sniff them — their fragrance is
   sweet perfume;
   taste the honey on each waxen bloom.
Sweetness and scent to your senses will steal
   and tell you that Hoya australis is real.

Cecilia Egan

Wax Flower

JUNE

1.

2.

3.

4.

5.

6.

7.

8.

9.

10.

11.

12.

13.

14.

15.

16.

JUNE

17.

18.

19.

20.

21.

22.

23.

24.

25.

26.

27.

28.

29.

30.

GREENHOOD
ORCHIDS

(Pterostylus.)

If you walk in the bush in Spring,
　　take care where you put your feet.
Look at the ground
　　where the small plants cling.
There you may see
　　a little green elf
　　deeply hooded to hide himself.

Tiny orchids are shy and quiet;
　　that's why they like to stay out
　　of sight.

Margaret Thornton
18/9/92

Greenhood Orchids

IVYLEAF VIOLET
(Viola hederacea)

Scalloped leaves in rosettes circled,
  Low I creep along the ground.
Thickly carpet damp dim gullies,
  Drier places, hardly found.

Wingback blossoms, arch neck dipping,
  Modest faces half revealed.
Petals white tipped, fine mauve
  bee paths,
  Guide to pollen near concealed.

Tendril tips the earth touch feeling,
  Tiny plantlets stitch afar.
Autumn seedy, my thin capsule, Pop!
  Explodes into a star.

Julia Thornton

Ivyleaf Violet

JULY

1.

2.

3.

4.

5.

6.

7.

8.

9.

10.

11.

12.

13.

14.

15.

16.

17.

18.

19.

20.

21.

22.

23.

24.

25.

26.

27.

28.

29.

30.

31.

BANKSIA
(Banksia spp.)

Banksia — small bush or graceful tree,
   in all its forms it's beautiful and strange,
   with fat, rough candle-flowers. And see
   serrated leaves in filigree pattern arranged,
   of sunlight and green, evanescent shadow.
Some say the many-lipped seedpods are ugly.
But, "Not so!" cry the fairies, "Not so!"
They house seed-babies
   in soft couches, snugly,
   until the seeds are ready for birth.
Then pod-mouths yawn and let them slide
   to earth.

Banksia

STURT'S DESERT PEA

(Clianthus formosus.)

The desert holds its secrets
   hidden in clay pans and dunes.
They bloom unknown to travellers
   in the clear light of the sun,
   and shining 'neath the moon.
One beauty is a great surprise —
   out in the empty land
   are garlands and crowns
   of magical flowers,
   black, purple and red,
   with grey, lacy leaves
   in a spiderweb bed.
The fairies fly from flower to flower
   giving kisses each happy hour.

Sturt's Desert Pea lives alone and remote
   dazzling the wilderness with its
   scarlet throat.

Margaret Thornton

Sturt's Desert Pea

AUGUST

1.

2.

3.

4.

5.

6.

7.

8.

9.

10.

11.

12.

13.

14.

15.

16.

AUGUST

17.

18.

19.

20.

21.

22.

23.

24.

25.

26.

27.

28.

29.

30.

31.

FRINGED LILY
(Thysonotus tuberosus)

Fringed lily, tiny dancer,
   who could believe that your skirts of mauve
   are not dream-woven, fringed by fantasy,
   sewn by fairy seamstresses
   from gossamer thin
   for fragile ballerinas to pirouette in?

Such a gorgeous dress is made
   for dance, for show and for parade!

Cecilia Egan

Fringed Lily

THE COMMON BUTTERCUP

(Ranunculus lappaceus)

True-born Australian buttercups do grow —
    a fact that not a lot of people know.
The satin surfaces of their five petals
    shine like the most precious of all metals.
But fairies, children and a few grown-ups
    know something else about our buttercups.
They know a way that you can surely tell
    if anyone likes butter really well.
The secret is to take a buttercup
    and hold it underneath his chin, close-up.
And if that chin reflects a golden-yellow,
    why then he is a butter-loving fellow!

(Buttercups hold magic butter, it is said.
The fairies spread it on their fairy bread.)

Cecilia Egan

The Common Buttercup

SEPTEMBER

1.

2.

3.

4.

5.

6.

7.

8.

9.

10.

11.

12.

13.

14.

15.

16.

SEPTEMBER

17.

18.

19.

20.

21.

22.

23.

24.

25.

26.

27.

28.

29.

30.

VICTORIAN CHRISTMAS BUSH

(Prostanthera lasianthos)

Some gardens smell of the bush —
*   the pungent fragrance comes in a rush.*
From where comes the haunting perfume?
No flowers to be seen, but dark green leaves
*   on the quiet little tree in the corner.*

Christmas comes — the quiet little tree
*   has been transformed by its fairy.*
No leaves to be seen, but snowywhite flowers,
*   lighting the land wherever it grows.*

The splendour declares
*   that Christmas is here.*

Margaret Thornton
22/9/92

Victorian Christmas Bush

NATIVE WISTERIA
(Hardenbergia comptoniana)

Climbing over bushes, trees and fences,
my twining stems
with leaves like long, green lances,
producing purple pea-flowers in masses,
are swings and slides
for fairy lads and lasses.

Cecilia Egan

Native Wisteria

OCTOBER

1.

2.

3.

4.

5.

6.

7.

8.

OCTOBER

9.

10.

11.

12.

13.

14.

15.

16.

OCTOBER

17.

18.

19.

20.

21.

22.

23.

24.

25.

26.

27.

28.

29.

30.

31.

KANGAROO PAW
(Anigosanthos spp.)

I am unusual — so is my name.
Out of Western Australia I came.
My quaint blooms show in
* Spring's bright, balmy weather —*
* orange, gold, or green and red together.*
I raise my hairy paws for you to see
* in garden beds — so please take care of me!*

Cecilia Egan

Kangaroo Paw

COMMON
PINK HEATH
(Epacris impressa)

Those brilliant hoods of startling pink
  springing on wild slopes and by the brink
  of paths, are bells no human hears —
  they only chime for fairy ears.
When tired of listening to the chimes,
  fairies wear them as hats sometimes.
And if a spell was cast on you,
  you'd hear pink heath's bells tinkling too,
  as fairies shake them in their secret dells —
  those tiny bonnets, those silent bells.

Cecilia Egan

Common Pink Heath

NOVEMBER

1.

2.

3.

4.

5.

6.

7.

8.

NOVEMBER

9.

10.

11.

12.

13.

14.

15.

16.

NOVEMBER

17.

18.

19.

20.

21.

22.

23.

24.

25.

26.

27.

28.

29.

30.

LILLY PILLY
(Acmena smithii)

Lovely tall and bushy Lilly Pilly
hides its fairies who are often silly,
gadding about amongst the berries
hanging from the trees like grapes
and cherries!

The boughs so strong and smooth grow evenly,
supporting the leaves and berries
on the tree —
a secret stairway for the little folk
who peep their shining faces
through its dark green cloak.

Shona Cornwall

Lilly Pilly

PINCUSHION HAKEA
(Hakea laurina)

Each plump and furry bud tightly embraces
a secret which brings joy to all the faces
of little kids. For, when our buds burst wide,
a pincushion, of all things, is inside!
A scarlet cushion, stuck with pins of gold,
but soft enough for little hands to hold.
Astonished little children laugh to see
such funny flowers growing on a tree!

Cecilia Egan

Pincushion Hakea

DECEMBER

1.

2.

3.

4.

5.

6.

7.

8.

DECEMBER

9.

10.

11.

12.

13.

14.

15.

16.

DECEMBER

17.

18.

19.

20.

21.

22.

23.

24.

25.

26.

27.

28.

29.

30.

31.

PIG FACE
(Carpobrotus spp.)

Why do they call me Pig Face? I don't know.
A dirty, grunting snout I never show!
Silk petals, boasting incandescent hues
  surround our gilded hearts — and these we use
  to hide our faces when the shadows reign.
But, come the sun, we show our smiles again!
We live on sandy dunes along the beach —
  for thirsty roots, fresh water's hard to reach.
Our leaves are juicy — "succulent", some say,
  which only means we store the rain away
  inside them, so that we can give a drink
  to silken flowers, yellow, mauve and pink.
Our colours are the brightest you will see,
  but "Pig Face"?
  I don't know — unless, maybe,
  if you've ever seen a dainty, newborn swine,
  you'd think his rosy face as sweet as mine!

Cecilia Egan

Pig Face

FOR MUM

Surrounded by poetry and flowers,
small children and little dogs:
this flower-fairy mother of ours.

Loving nature, words and fantasy,
you were the obvious choice
to write the gentle fairy poems
and give the flowers voice.

Haunting music, painful as grieving,
sweet as love; a gift from Shona,
you hear as your mind is word-weaving.

The comforts in your days now
are gifts from Julia's heart.
As you gave to us, so we give to you,
and this verse is Celia's part.